Just Behave, Pablo Picasso

BY JONAH WINTER

PICTURES BY KEVIN HAWKES

ARTHUR A. LEVINE BOOKS
An Imprint of Scholastic Inc.

ONE DAY the world is a peaceful, lovely landscape painting. . . .

The next day — **BLAM!** — Pablo bursts through the canvas, paintbrush in hand, ready to paint something fresh and new.

Painting pictures is as easy for Pablo as eating — and even more **FUN.**

In art class, he is surrounded by students twice his age. In the time it takes them to do a sketch, Pablo has completed a large oil painting.

In the time it takes other people to admire the *exquisite* beauty
of his art, young Pablo has moved on to some other style . . .

. . . to some other country, even! Today, he lives in Spain and wears the cape of a bullfighter.

Tomorrow, he lives in Paris and wears a beret — *ooh la la!*

Always on the go, always changing, today he paints blue paintings because he feels blue.

But tomorrow, Pablo paints rose-colored paintings because he feels rose colored. The gallery owner says,

C'EST MAGNIFIQUE!

"Paint about two hundred more paintings **JUST LIKE THAT!**"

Pablo does, and people love him, and suddenly he's
Mr. Big Famous Art Star: **PABLO PICASSO**.
Picasso this, Picasso that —

Picasso, Picasso, Picasso!

One day he's starving, the next day he's rich and
famous. That's great, but . . .

Pablo gets bored painting rose-colored paintings. He longs to paint something new, something different. Lost in a cloud of his own imagination, Pablo goes wandering.

As if in a dream, he floats through Paris, arriving at last at an art show of African masks. His eyes get big. He is seeing something new for the first time.

These masks . . . they do not look like real faces. But they seem to have some magical, wonderful power that realistic paintings do not have.

This gives Pablo an idea. Back at his studio, he begins a new painting, unlike anything he's ever done before.

He paints and he paints, unable to stop. He does not let people see what he's painting. They must wait till it's finished! He's so excited he can barely speak . . . !

The day arrives. The painting is unveiled. It's different from any other painting in the world — the faces and bodies don't even look real. They look like African masks.

Ugly? Terrible? **This hurts Pablo's feelings. He is so proud of his new painting — how could people be so mean? This makes Pablo mad. All anyone wants is for him to keep painting the same old picture, over and over. Well, guess what? He doesn't want to, he doesn't have to, and he's not going to! HAH!**

29

Back in his studio, Pablo starts working on something even more outlandish than his last painting.

"Why can't you keep painting beautiful pictures?" asks his wife. "Why can't you keep making art that makes sense?"

"The world today doesn't make sense," says Pablo. "Why should I make pictures that do?"

And sure enough, much of the world around Pablo doesn't make sense. Everything is changing all the time. New things are being invented: cars, airplanes, telephones, bombs.

"But Pablo," says a fellow artist, "your new painting doesn't look real."

"Everything you can imagine," says Pablo, "is real." And sure enough, the crazy shapes and images you see when you close your eyes are very much a part of you, just as real as what you see with open eyes.

"You should go back to painting just like you used to,"
says a chorus of art dealers. "That's where the money is."
Picasso stands on his rooftop, defiant, and yells back,
"To copy yourself is pathetic!"

"Why are you doing this?" shouts another chorus of friends and family, for they know he is at work on something even more outlandish. "It doesn't make any sense!"

Picasso expands himself to a height of one hundred feet and shouts,

Suddenly, everyone in Paris opens their windows at once and shouts,

But, like a soldier down in his bunker, Pablo ignores all the voices of his enemies. He keeps on painting the painting he wants to paint, even though he knows many people will hate it, call it ugly, and say mean things to

him — even meaner than what they've already said. And when the painting is done, it's so different, so new, so abstract, so *modern* . . . that for a few minutes, no one knows *what* to say!

Later on, people say Pablo Picasso is the first modern artist. They say he is a force of nature, that he is courageous, that he is the most original artist of his time. And they say so to this day.

Pablo Picasso

Pablo Picasso is perhaps the most famous artist of the twentieth century. He was born on October 25, 1881, in Spain, but when he grew up he moved to France, where he lived and worked on and off until his death on April 8, 1973. By his last year, at the age of ninety-one, Picasso had gone through several artistic styles and created thousands upon thousands of paintings, drawings, prints, and sculptures. This book is about an early period in Picasso's life, during his twenties, when he created a bold new style of art called "Cubism," which showed things as they would look if you could see them from several different angles at once, using brushstrokes that looked like cubes. As an artistic style, Cubism was the most important step ever taken from making "realistic" pictures to "abstract" ones in European art. In some Cubist paintings, it's hard to even tell that there is an object or a person as the subject — that's how abstract they look.

To be fair, Picasso had some major help in creating this new style from his friend Georges Braque, who was also a great artist and is now regarded as the cocreator of Cubism. The two of them worked side by side for years and influenced each other greatly. But it was Picasso who painted the first painting that began to inspire Cubism. It was called *Les Demoiselles d'Avignon*, and it is the painting that people in this story call "ugly" and "terrible." The painting at the very end of the book, *Girl with a Mandolin*, though not officially the "first" Cubist painting, is nonetheless one of the first major Cubist paintings and a perfect example of this new style.

What's amazing about Picasso is not just that he, despite terrible criticism, started a whole new kind of art, and a whole new way of looking at the world — an act that took courage and brilliance and is the subject of this book. What's as amazing is that he kept coming up with new styles, new ways of seeing, all the way to the end of his life. He painted one of his most famous paintings, *Guernica*, when he was fifty-five years old. And even as a very old man, he had the energy, the enthusiasm, and the curiosity of a young child. Love him or hate him (he is both loved and hated), it is impossible to ignore Pablo Picasso and what he did for — and to — art.

The paintings in this book

pg. 9: *Girl with Bare Feet*, 1895, Musée National Picasso, Paris, France

pp 10–11:

1) *Dona Maria*, 1896, Museu Picasso, Barcelona, Spain

2) *Science and Charity*, 1897, Museu Picasso, Barcelona, Spain

3) *Pio Baroja*, 1901, Private collection

4) *The Old Fisherman*, 1895, Museu de Montserrat, Barcelona, Spain

5) *Decadent Poet*, 1900, Museu Picasso, Barcelona, Spain

6) *Menu of Els Ouatre Gats*, 1899–1900, Museu Picasso, Barcelona, Spain

7) *Spanish Couple in Front of an Inn*, 1900, Kawamura Memorial Museum of Art, Sakura, Japan

8) *Poster Design for Dramas Criollos*, 1900, Nationalgalerie, Berlin, Germany

pp 12–13: *Bullfight*, 1900, Private collection

pp 16–17:

1) *Woman With a Helmet of Hair*, 1904, The Art Institute of Chicago, Chicago, Illinois, USA

2) *Couple*, 1904, Private collection

3) *Self Portrait with Cloak*, 1901, Musée National Picasso, Paris, France

4) *Woman Ironing*, 1904, Solomon R. Guggenheim Museum, New York, New York, USA

5) *The Blue Room*, 1904, The Phillips Collection, Washington, DC, USA

6) *Portrait of Suzanne Bloch*, 1904, São Paulo Museum of Art, São Paulo, Brazil

pg. 19: *The Actor*, 1904–1905, The Metropolitan Museum of Art, New York, New York, USA

pp 26–27: *Les Desmoiselles d'Avignon*, 1907, The Museum of Modern Art, New York, New York, USA

pp 42–43, 44: *Girl with a Mandolin*, 1910, The Museum of Modern Art, New York, New York, USA

pg. 46: *Bull's Head*, 1942, Musée National Picasso, Paris, France

pg. 48: *Bullfight*, detail from Picasso's sketchbook, c. 1890, Museu Picasso, Barcelona, Spain

Published by Arthur A. Levine
Books, an imprint of Scholastic Inc.,
Publishers since 1920. SCHOLASTIC and
the LANTERN LOGO are trademarks and/or
registered trademarks of Scholastic Inc.

Library of Congress Cataloging-in-Publication Data
Winter, Jonah, 1962–
Just behave, Pablo Picasso! / by Jonah Winter ; pictures by Kevin Hawkes.
p. cm.   ISBN 978-0-545-13291-6 (hardcover : alk. paper) 1. Picasso,
Pablo, 1881-1973—Juvenile literature. I. Picasso, Pablo, 1881-1973. II.
Hawkes, Kevin. III. Title.
ND553.P5W54 2012   709.2—dc23   2011026234
10 9 8 7 6 5 4 3 2 1   12 13 14 15 16
First edition, February 2012 • Printed in Singapore 46
The art for this book was created using open acrylics
and sepia pencil on paper. Book design by David Saylor

FOR SOFIA CORPORAN AND HER STUDENTS
(PAST, PRESENT, AND FUTURE) — JW

TO SPENCER AND SAM — KH

48